W9-DIN-138

1895
BdT

JE

COMICS LAND

by
STONE ARCH
BOOKS

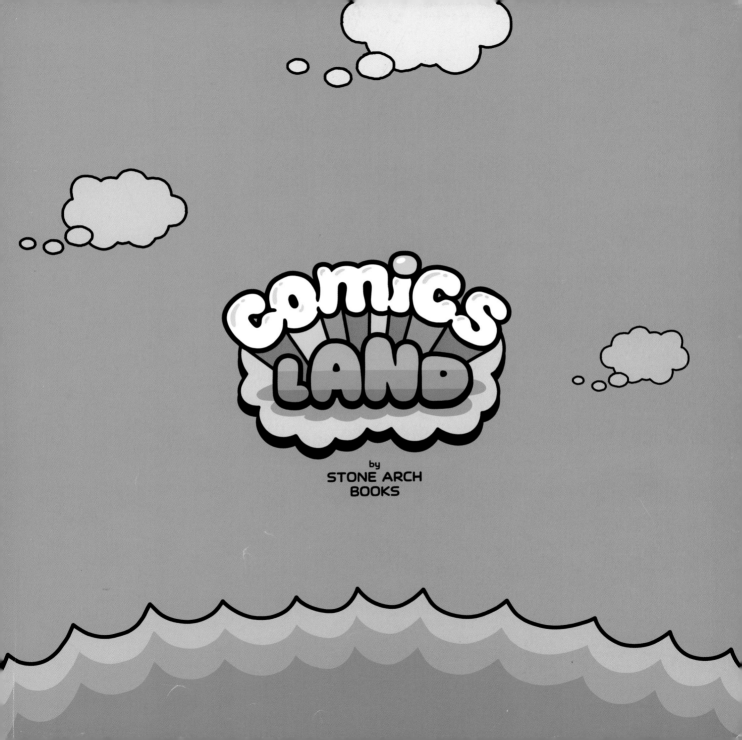

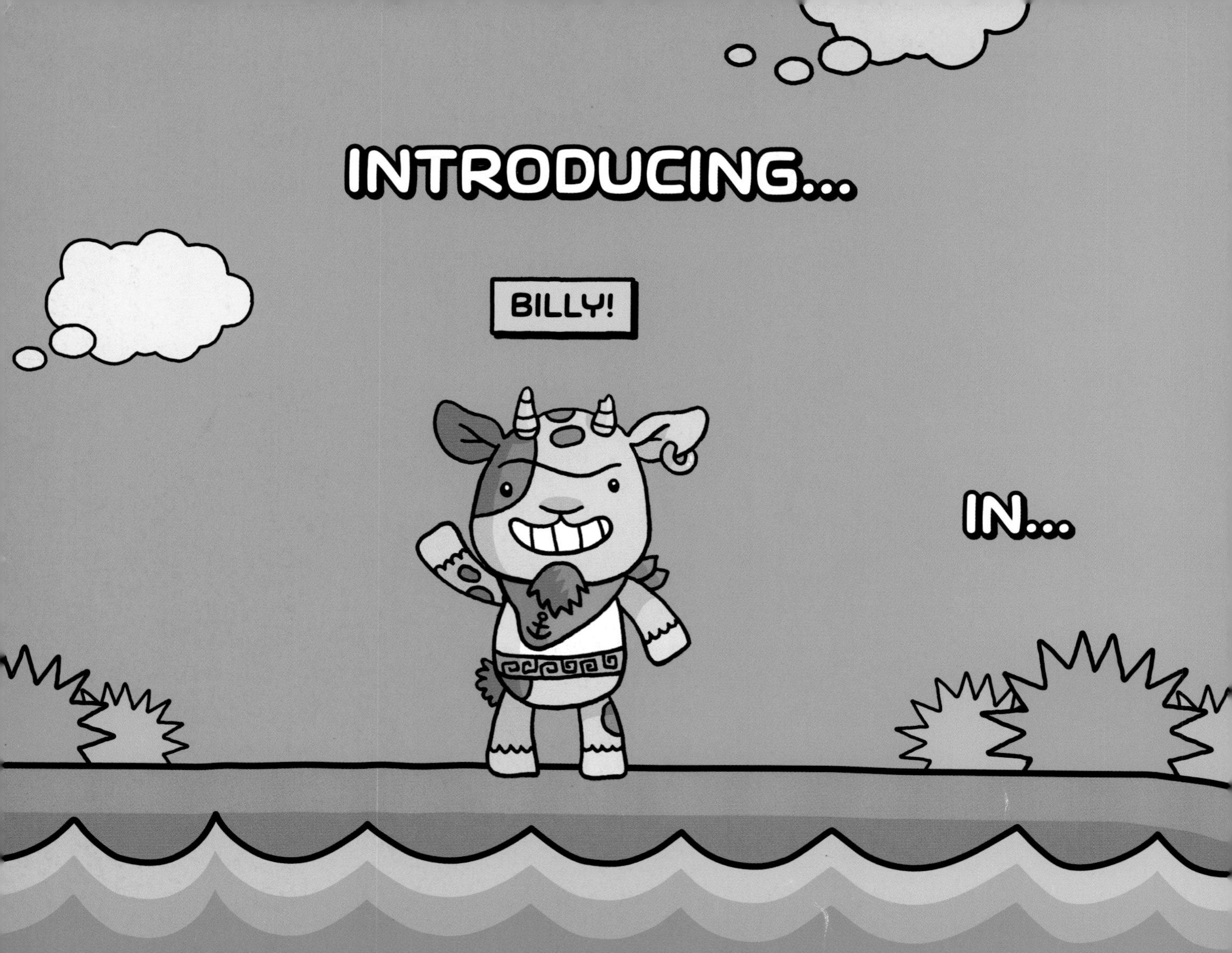
INTRODUCING...
BILLY!
IN...

STONE ARCH BOOKS™
www.capstonepub.com

1710 Roe Crest Drive, North Mankato, Minnesota 56003

Cataloging-in-Publication data is available on the Library of Congress website.
ISBN: 978-1-4342-6282-0 (hardcover) • ISBN: 978-1-4342-4944-9 (library binding) •
ISBN: 978-1-4342-6429-9 (ebook)

Printed in China by Nordica.
0413/CA21300423
032013 007226NORDF13

GOAT ON A BOAT

written by
JOHN SAZAKLIS

illustrated by
JESS BRADLEY

designed by
BOB LENTZ

edited by
JULIE GASSMAN

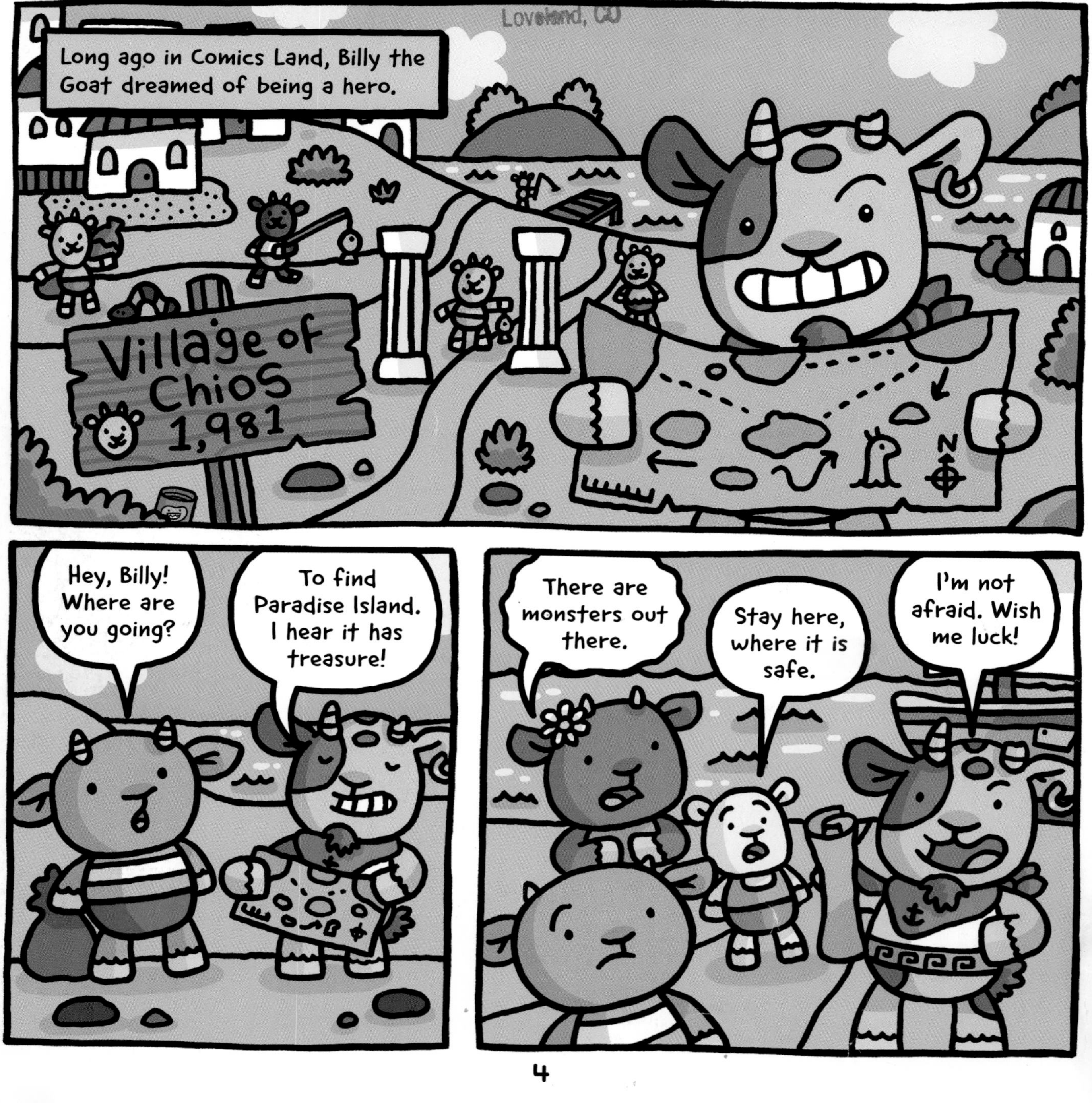
Long ago in Comics Land, Billy the Goat dreamed of being a hero.
Village of Chios 1,981
Hey, Billy! Where are you going?
To find Paradise Island. I hear it has treasure!
There are monsters out there.
Stay here, where it is safe.
I'm not afraid. Wish me luck!

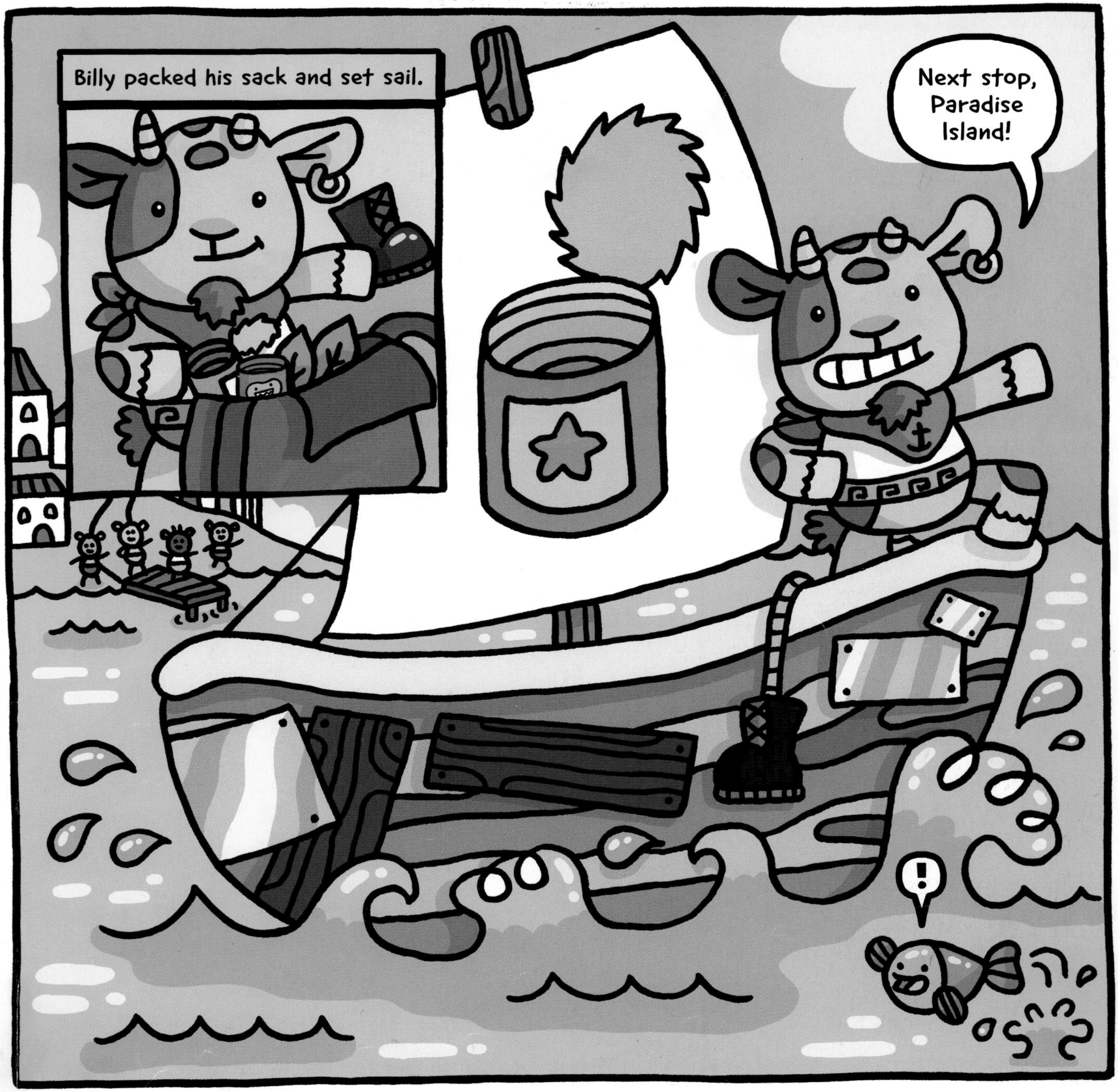
Billy packed his sack and set sail.
Next stop, Paradise Island!

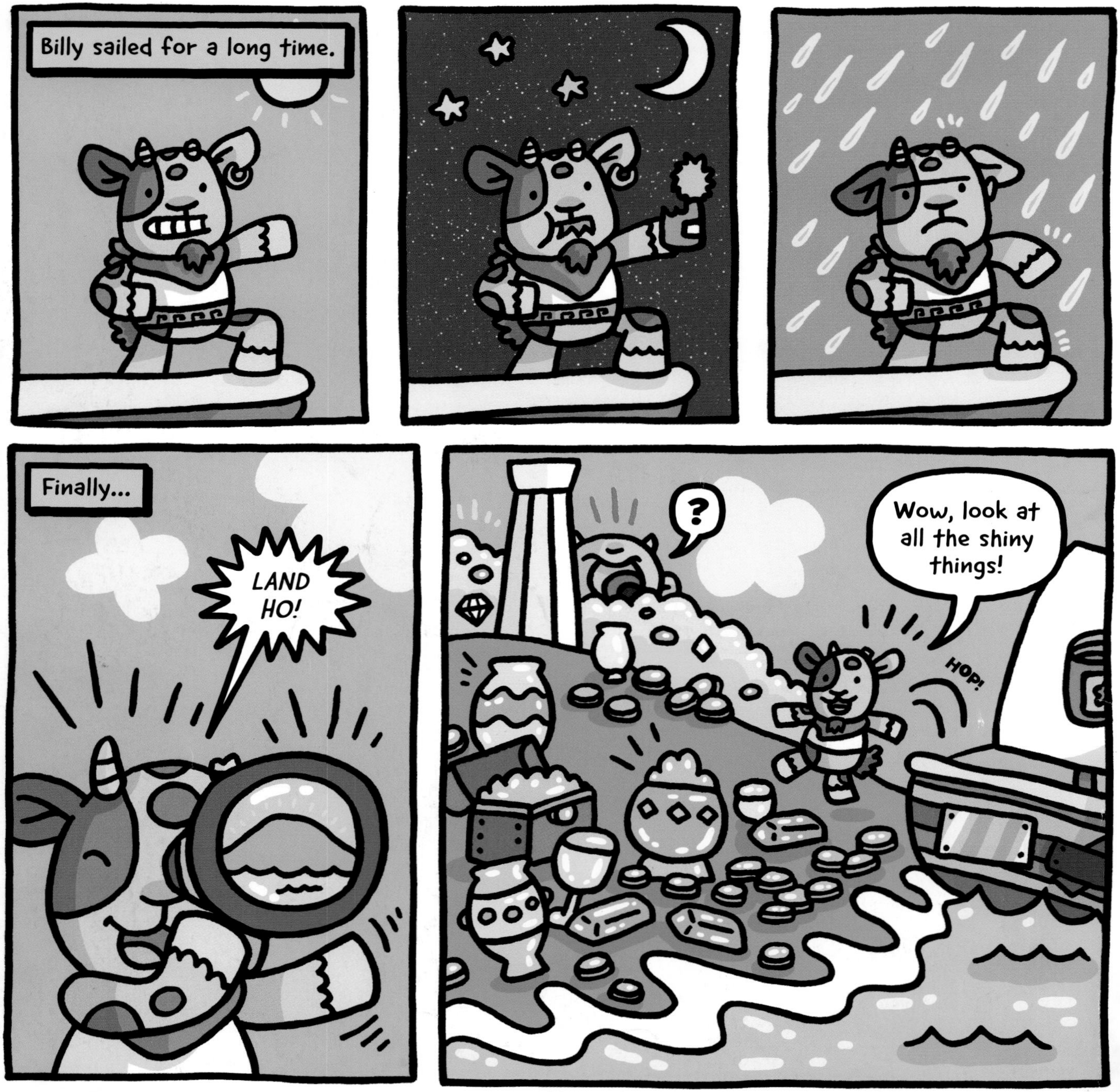

Billy sailed for a long time.
Finally...
LAND HO!
?
Wow, look at all the shiny things!
HOP!

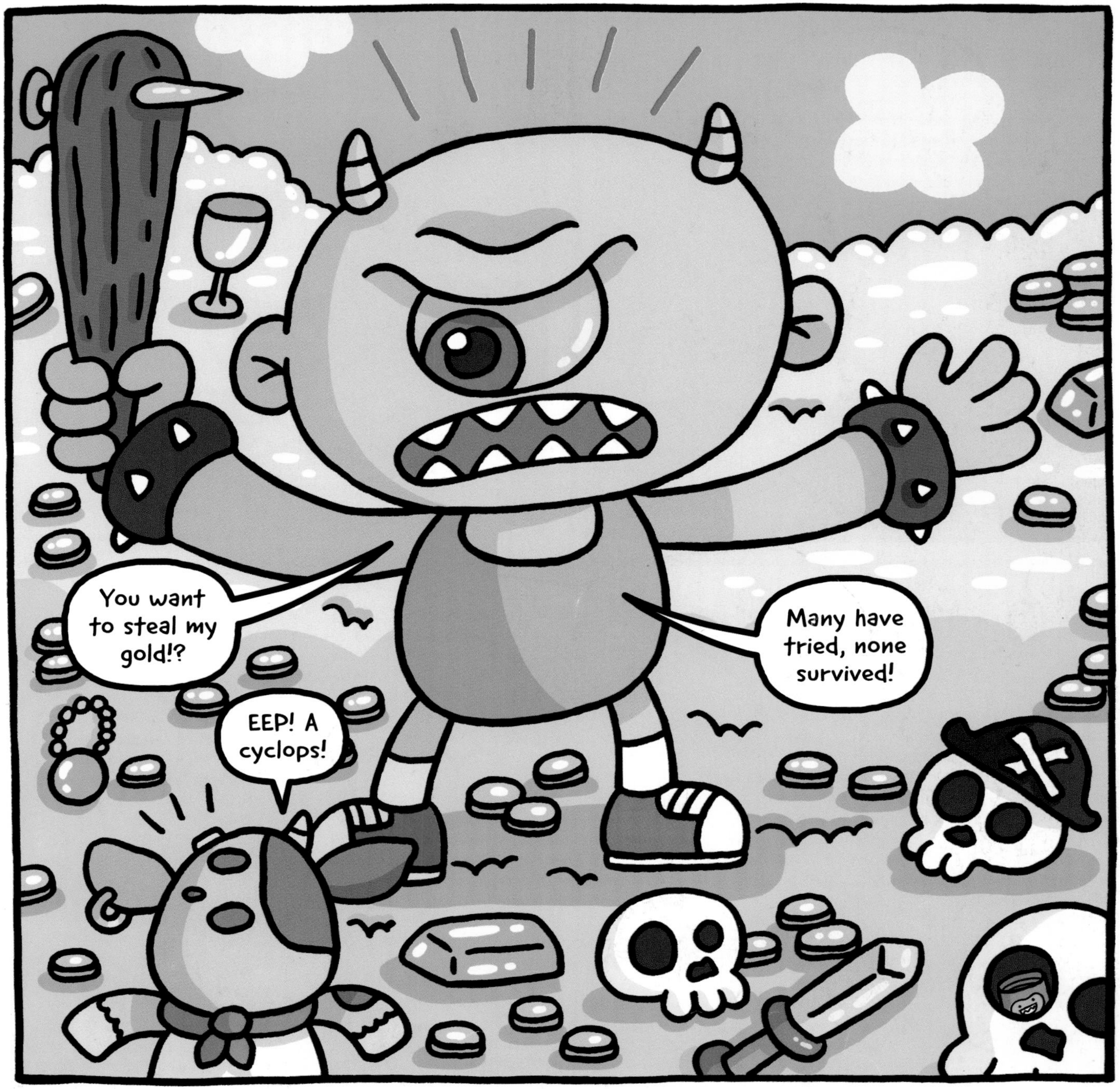
You want to steal my gold!?
EEP! A cyclops!
Many have tried, none survived!

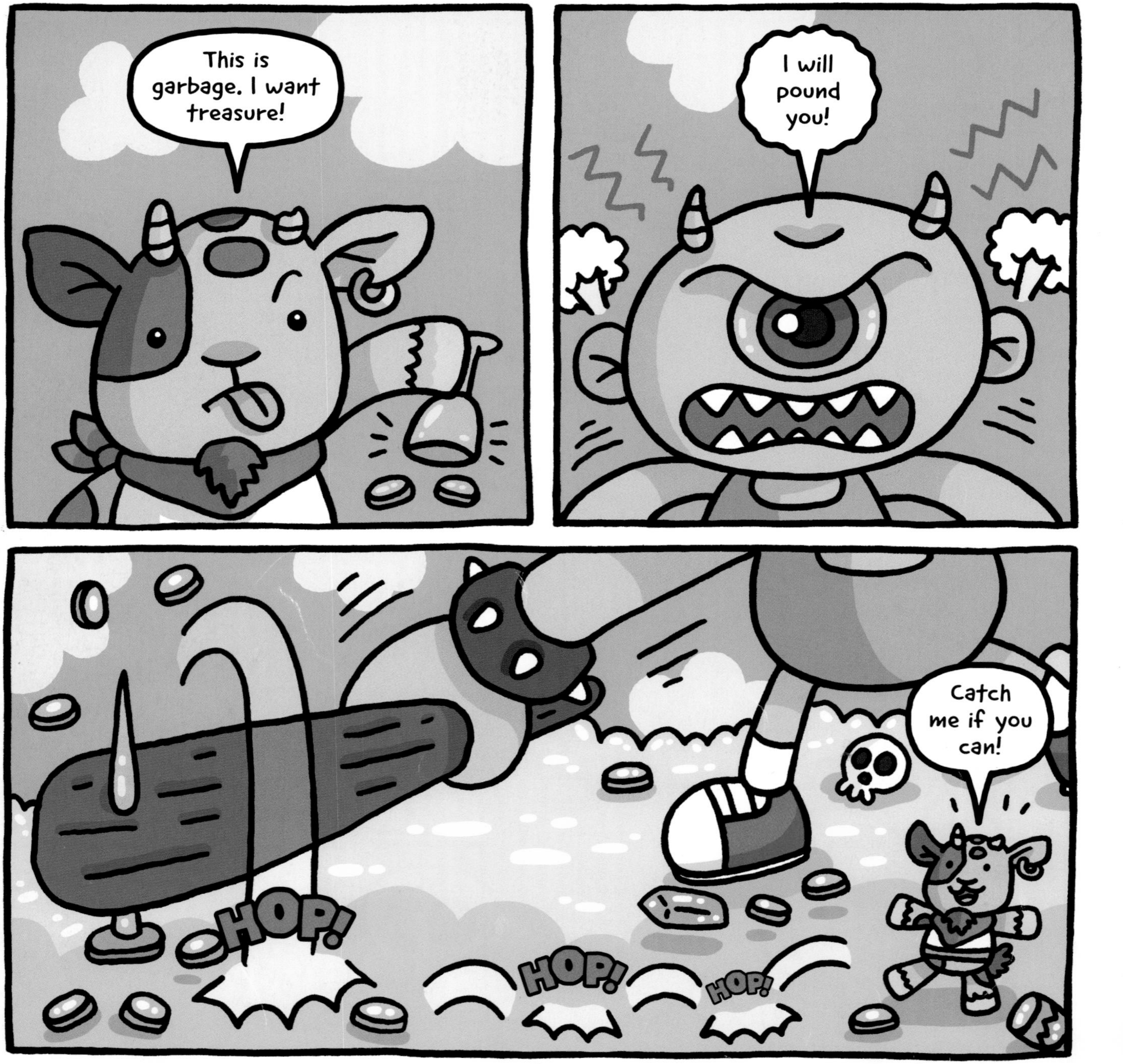
This is garbage. I want treasure!
I will pound you!
Catch me if you can!
HOP!
HOP!
HOP!

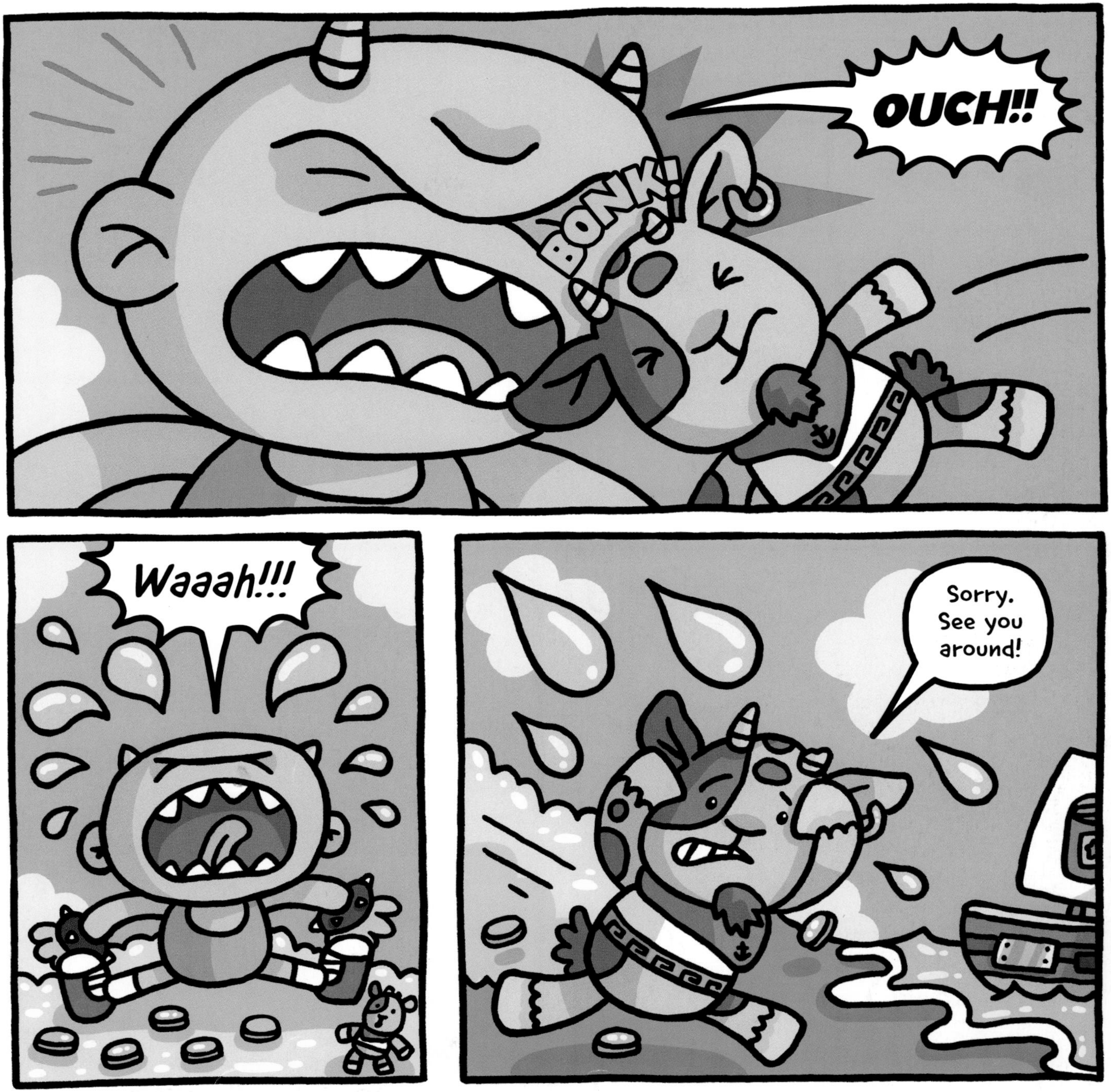
OUCH!!
BONK!
Waaah!!!
Sorry. See you around!

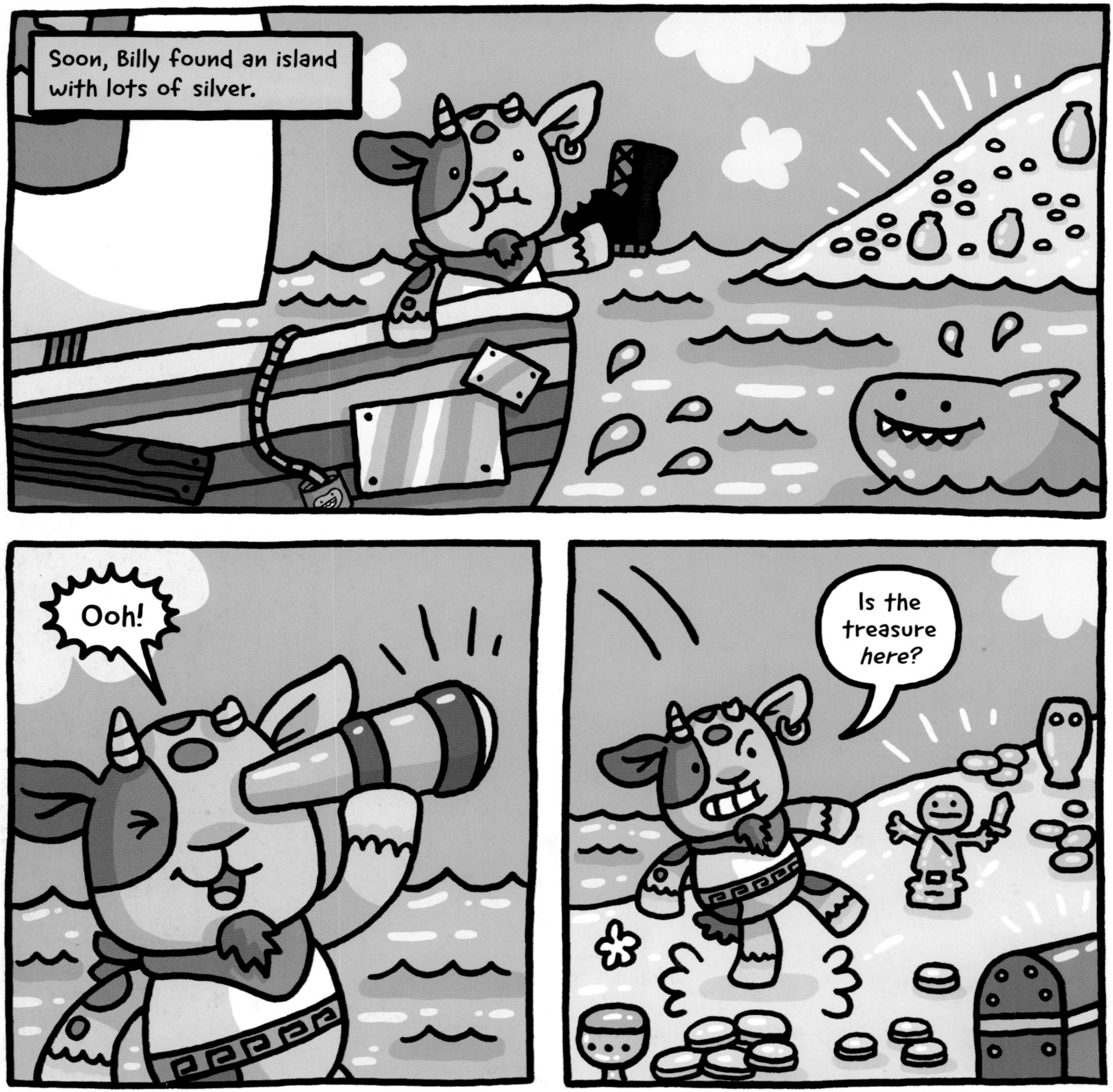
Soon, Billy found an island with lots of silver.
Ooh!
Is the treasure *here*?

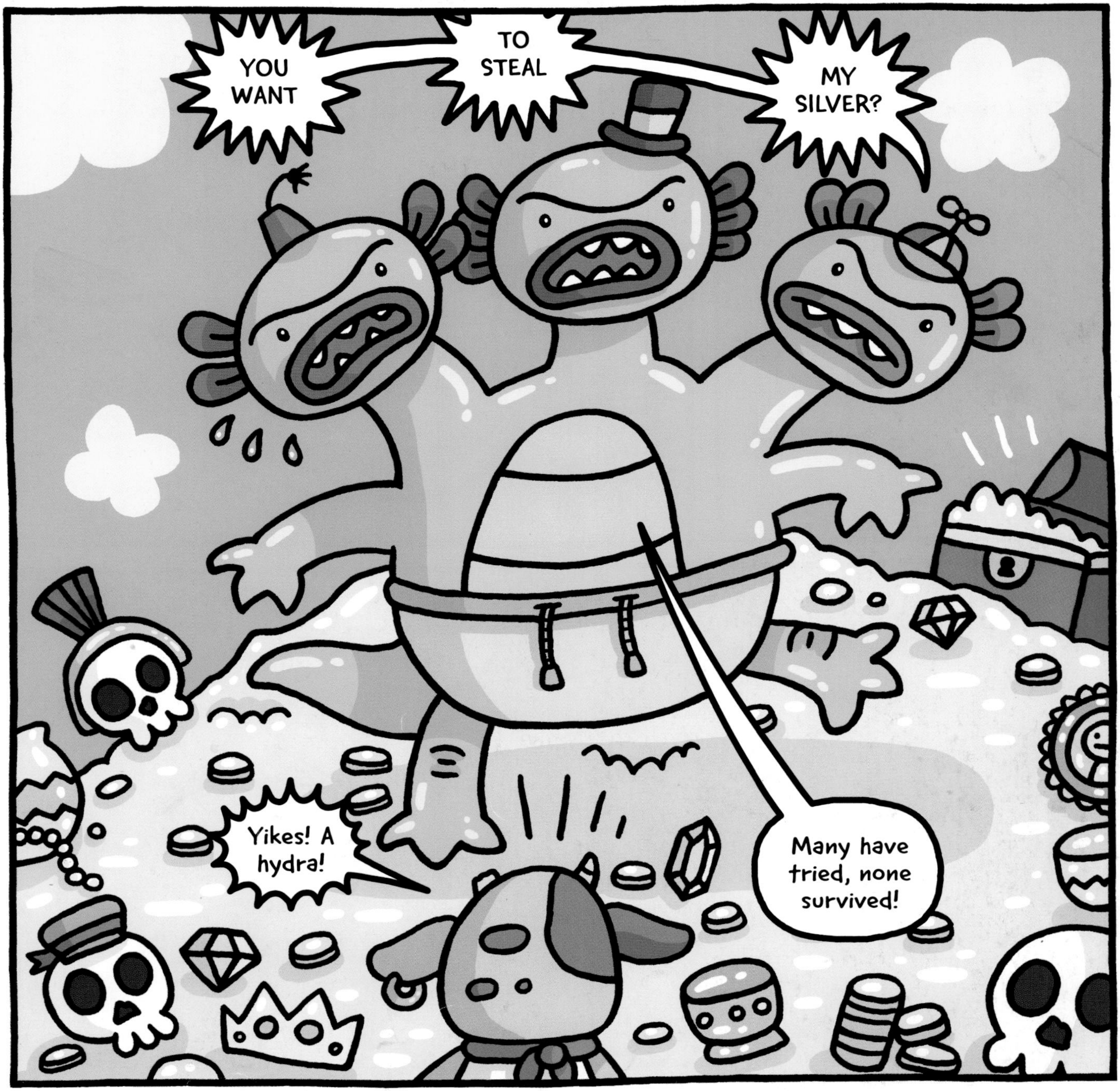
YOU WANT
TO STEAL
MY SILVER?
Yikes! A hydra!
Many have tried, none survived!

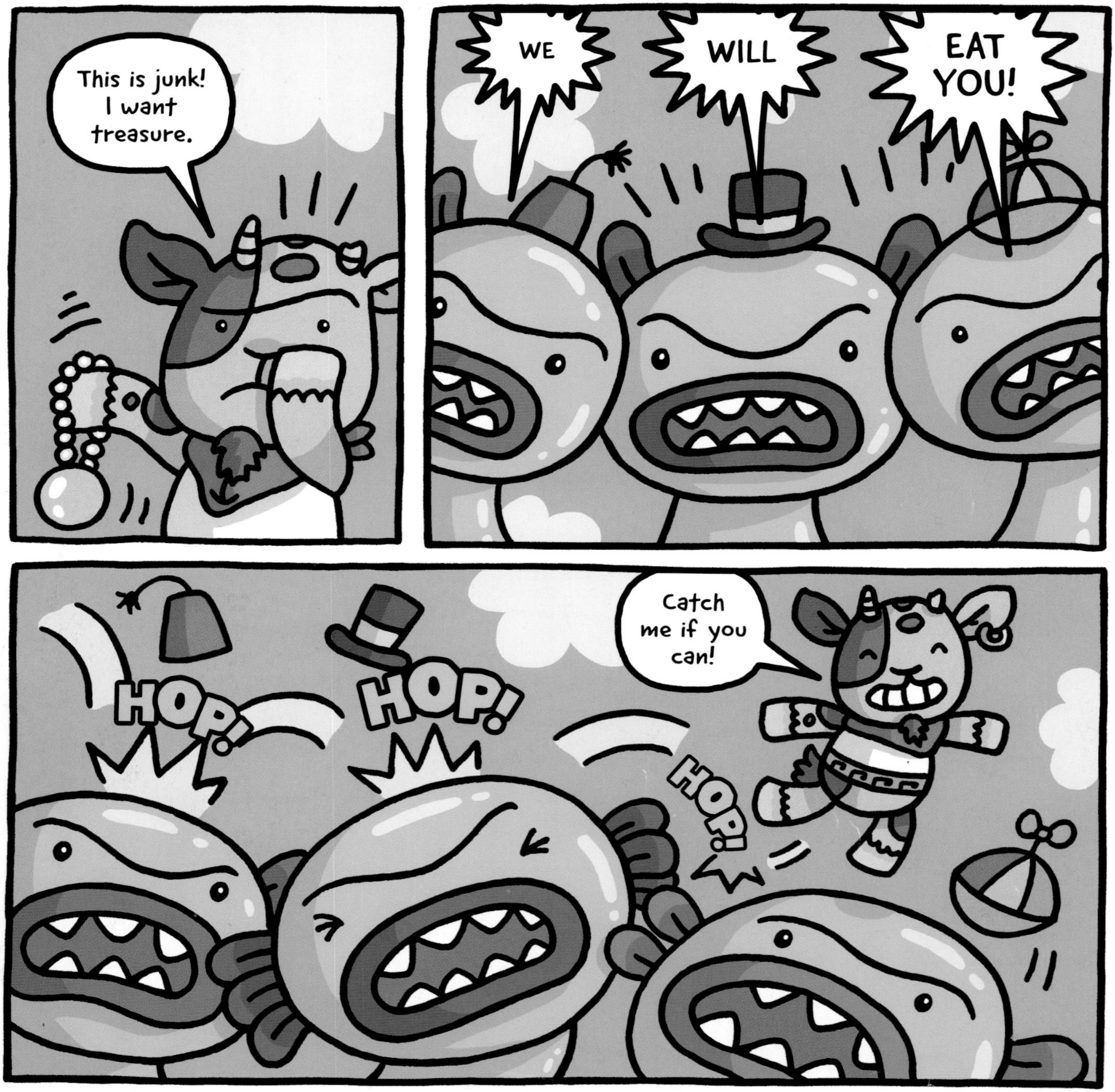
This is junk! I want treasure.
WE
WILL
EAT YOU!
HOP!
HOP!
HOP!
Catch me if you can!

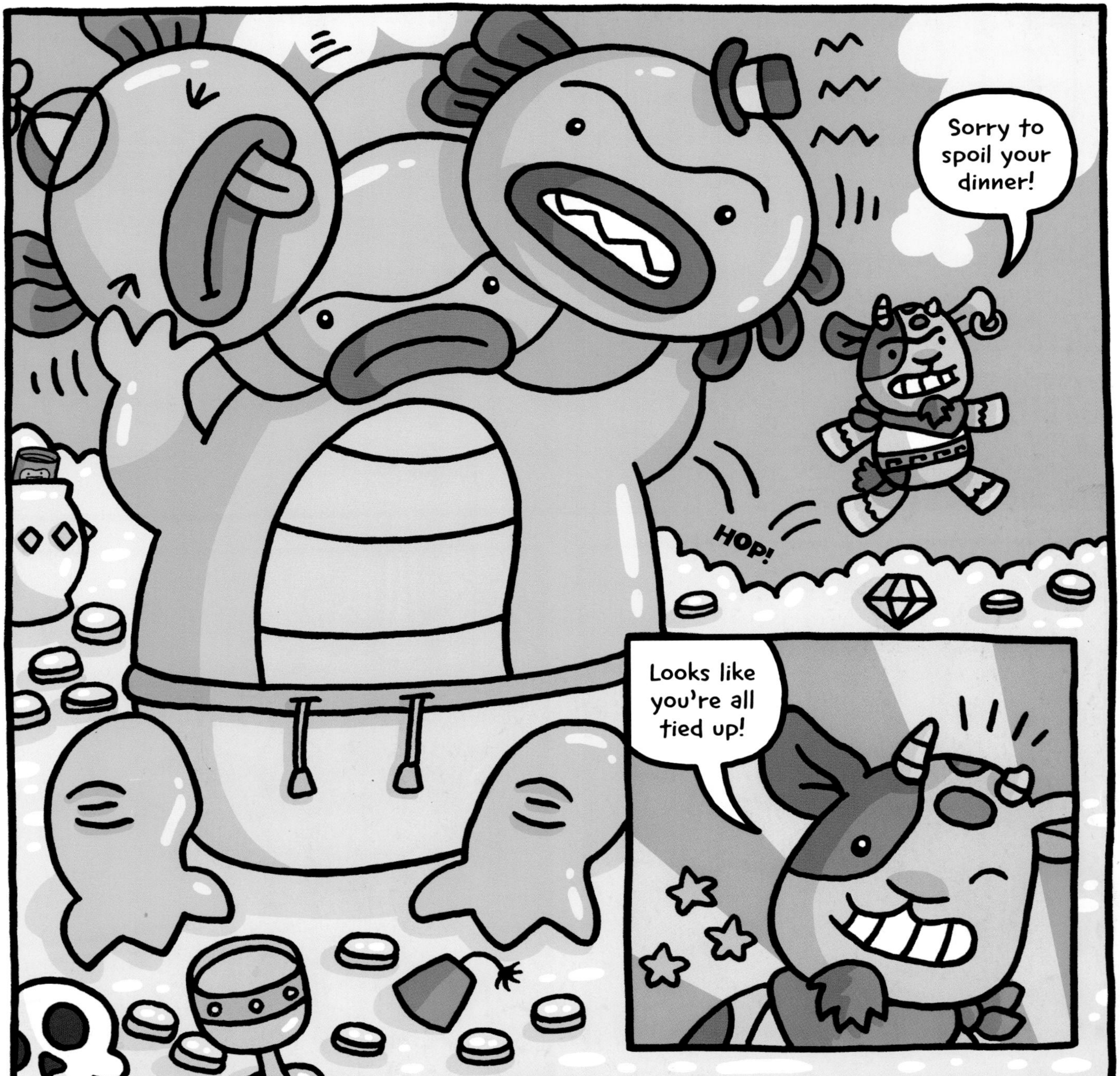
Sorry to spoil your dinner!
HOP!
Looks like you're all tied up!

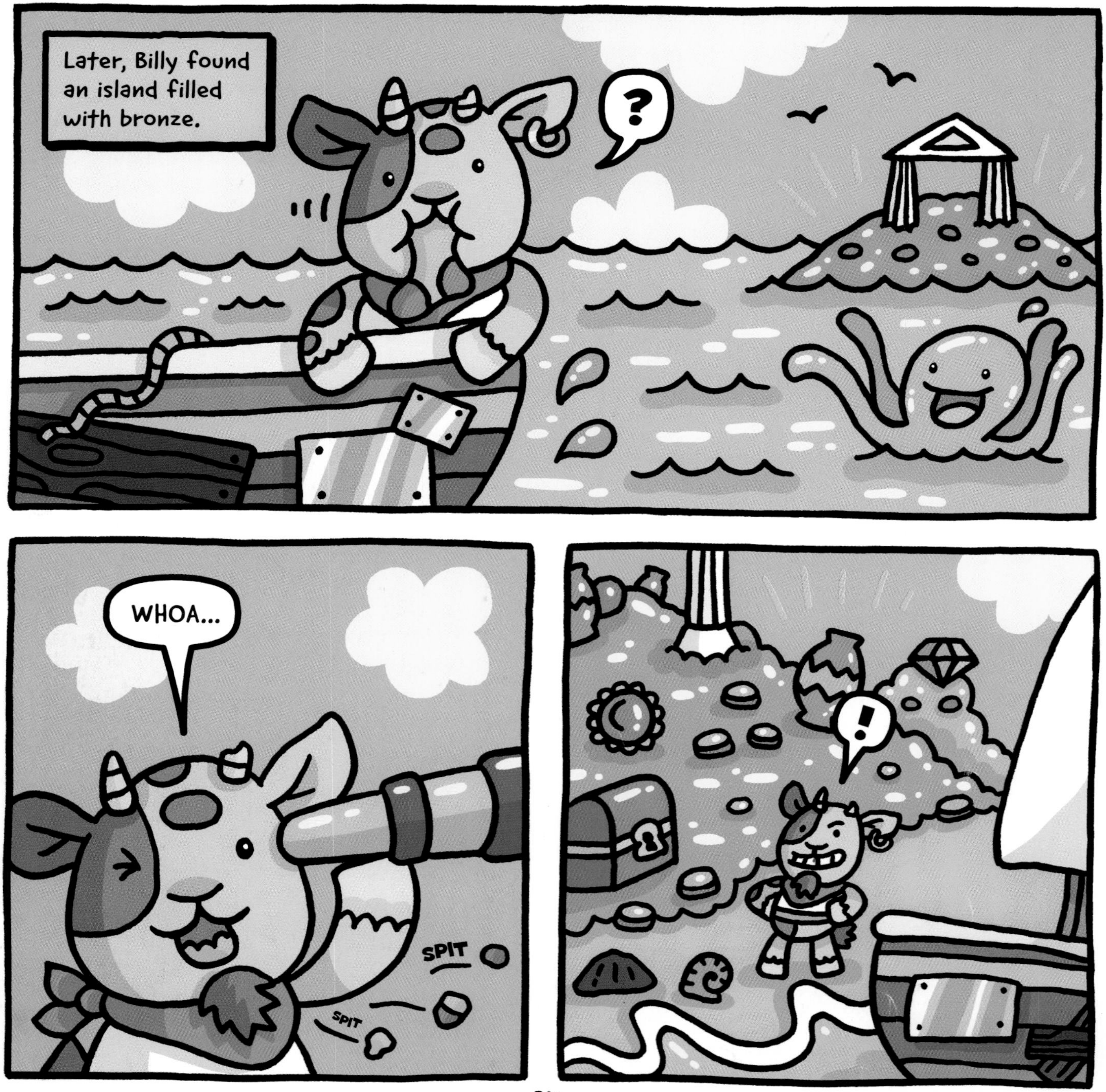
Later, Billy found an island filled with bronze.
?
WHOA...
SPIT
SPIT
!

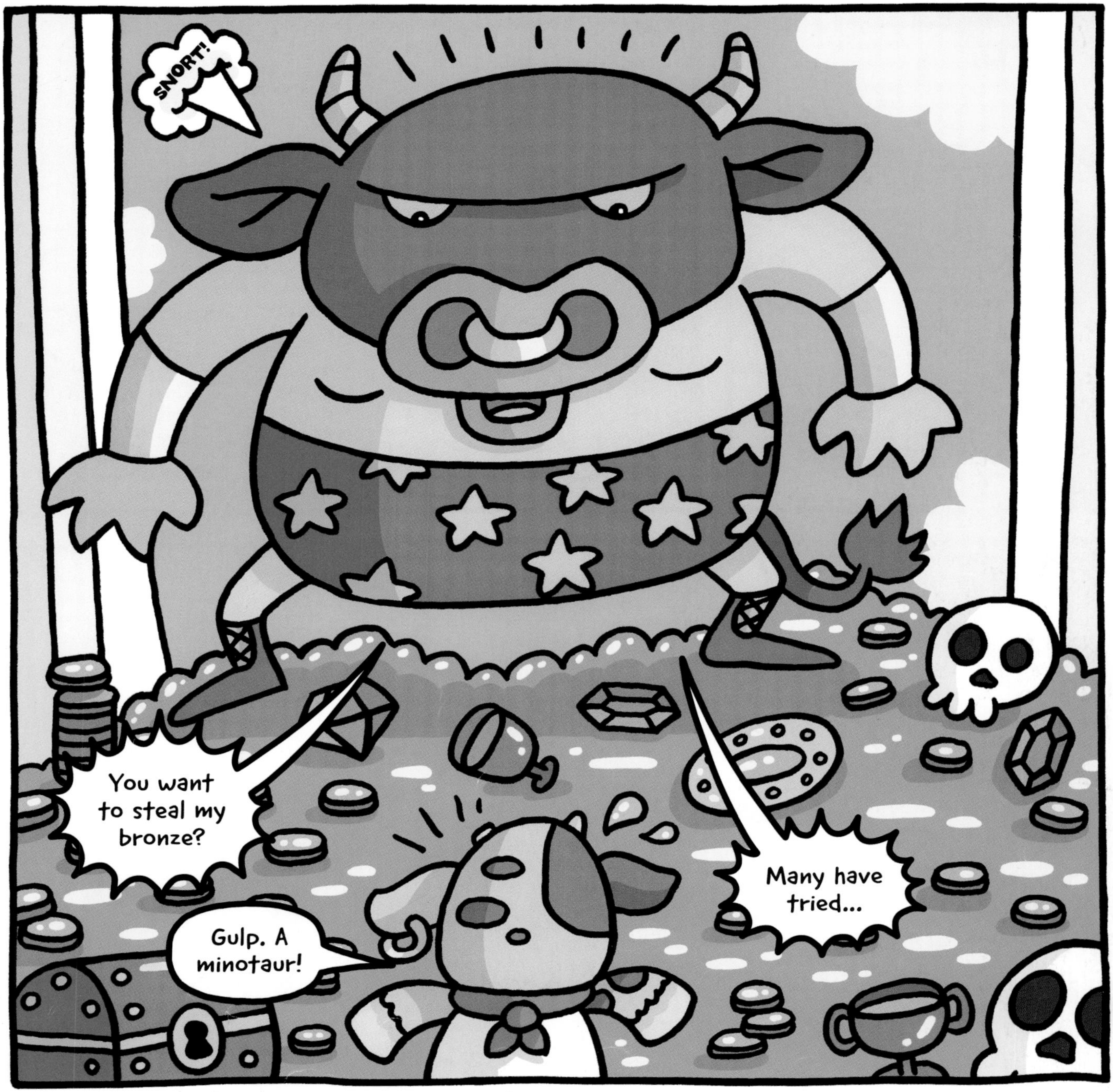
SNORT!
You want to steal my bronze?
Many have tried...
Gulp. A minotaur!

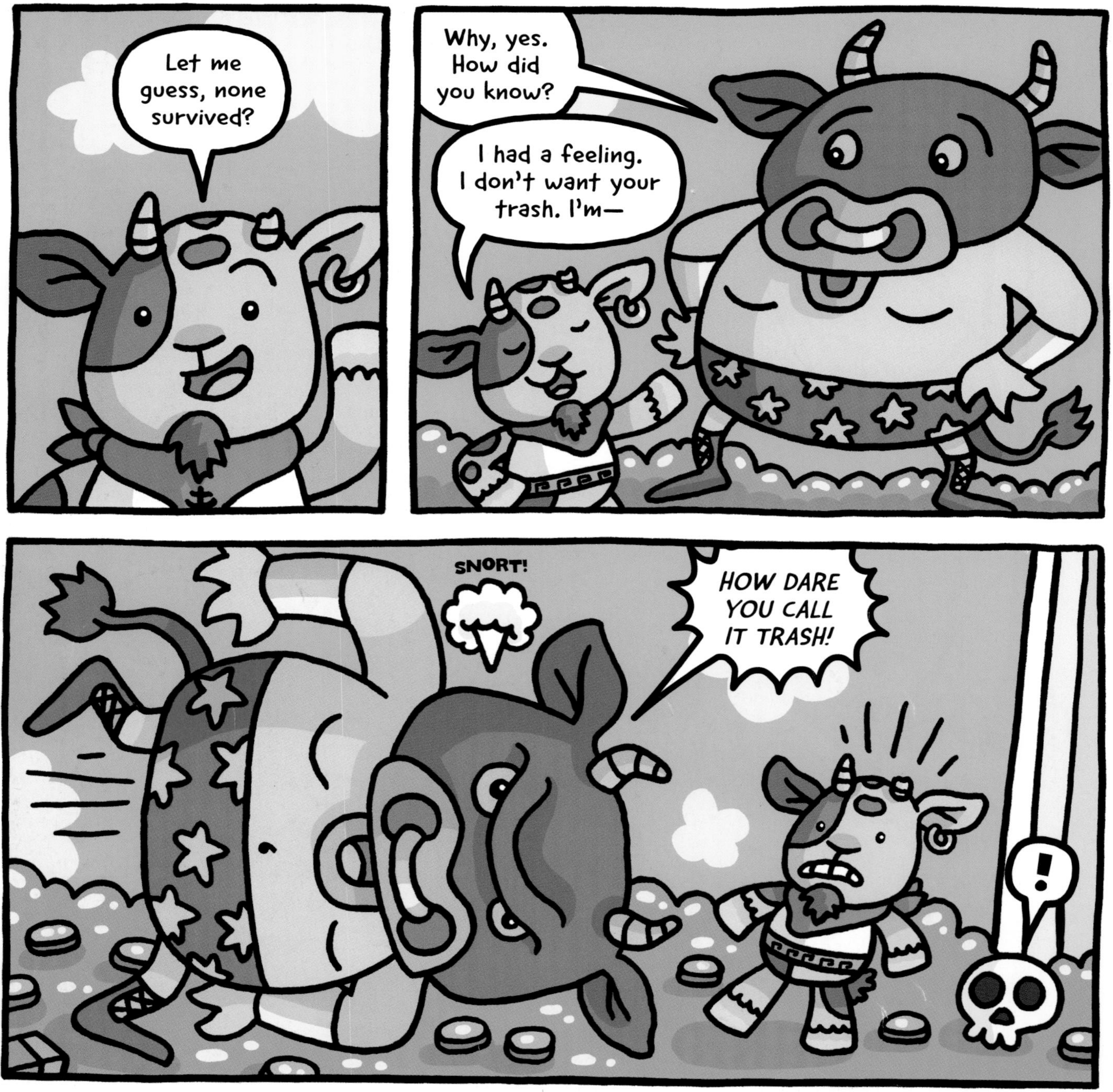
Let me guess, none survived?
Why, yes. How did you know?
I had a feeling. I don't want your trash. I'm—
SNORT!
HOW DARE YOU CALL IT TRASH!
!

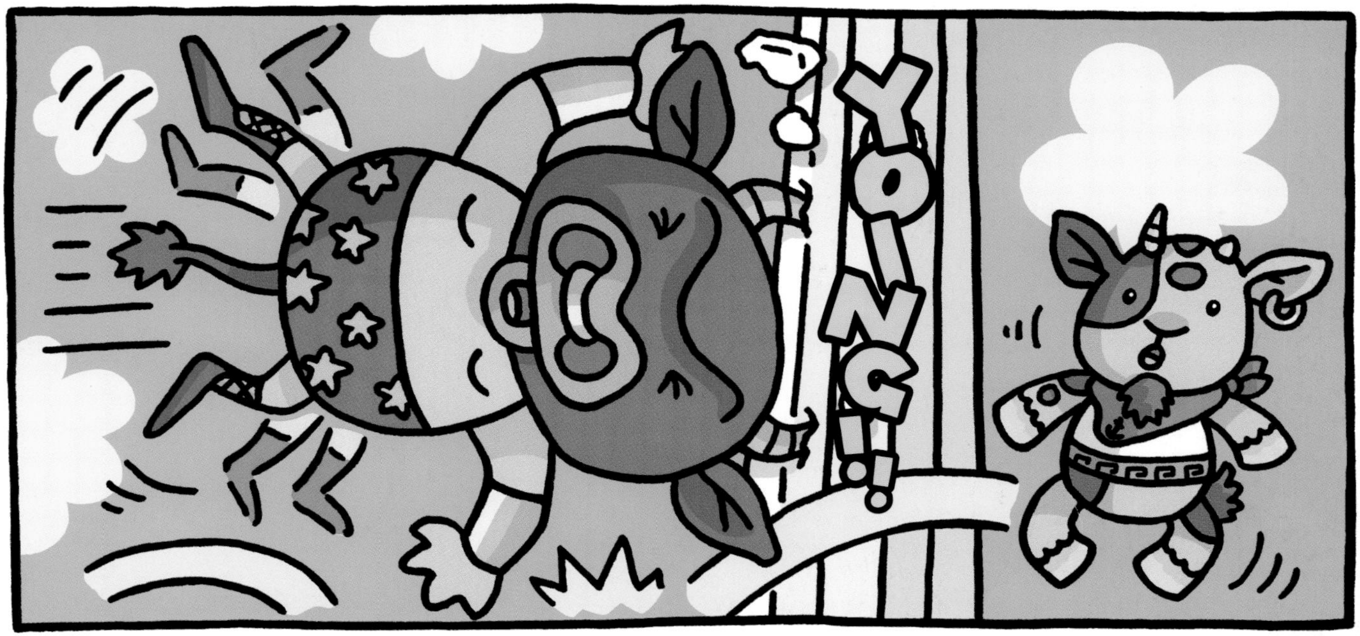
YOING!!

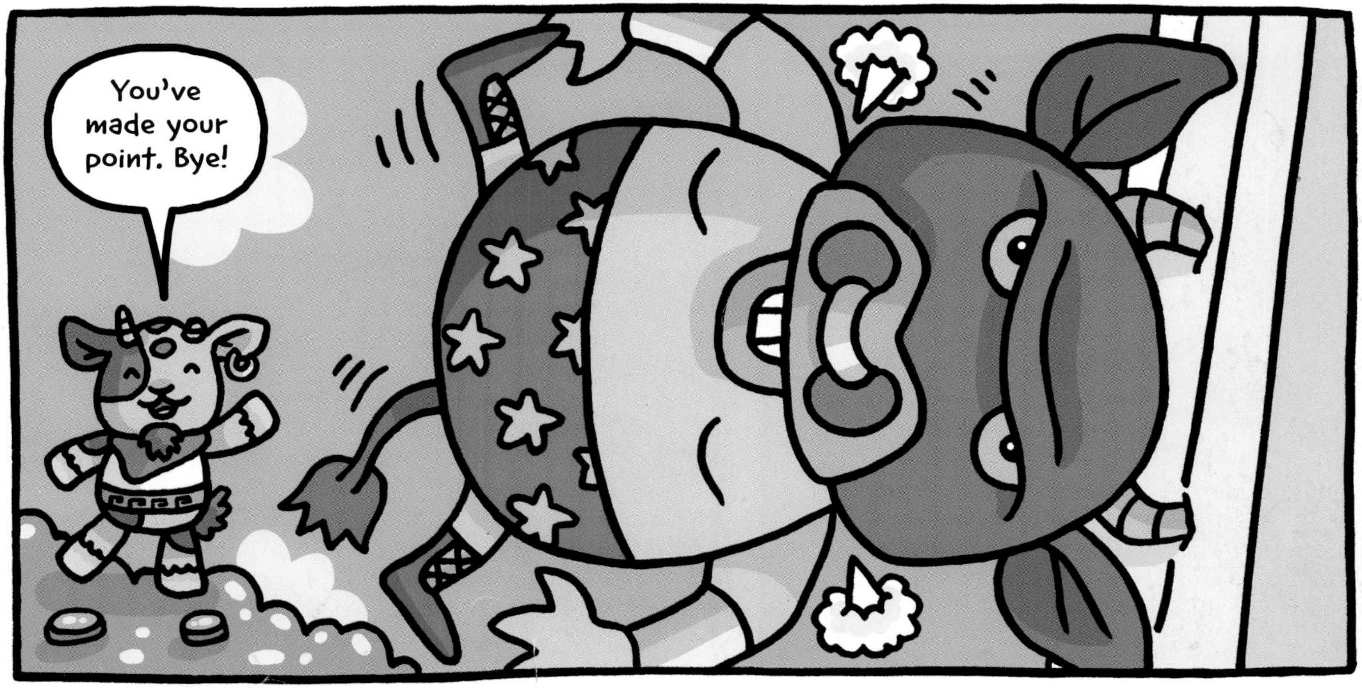
You've made your point. Bye!

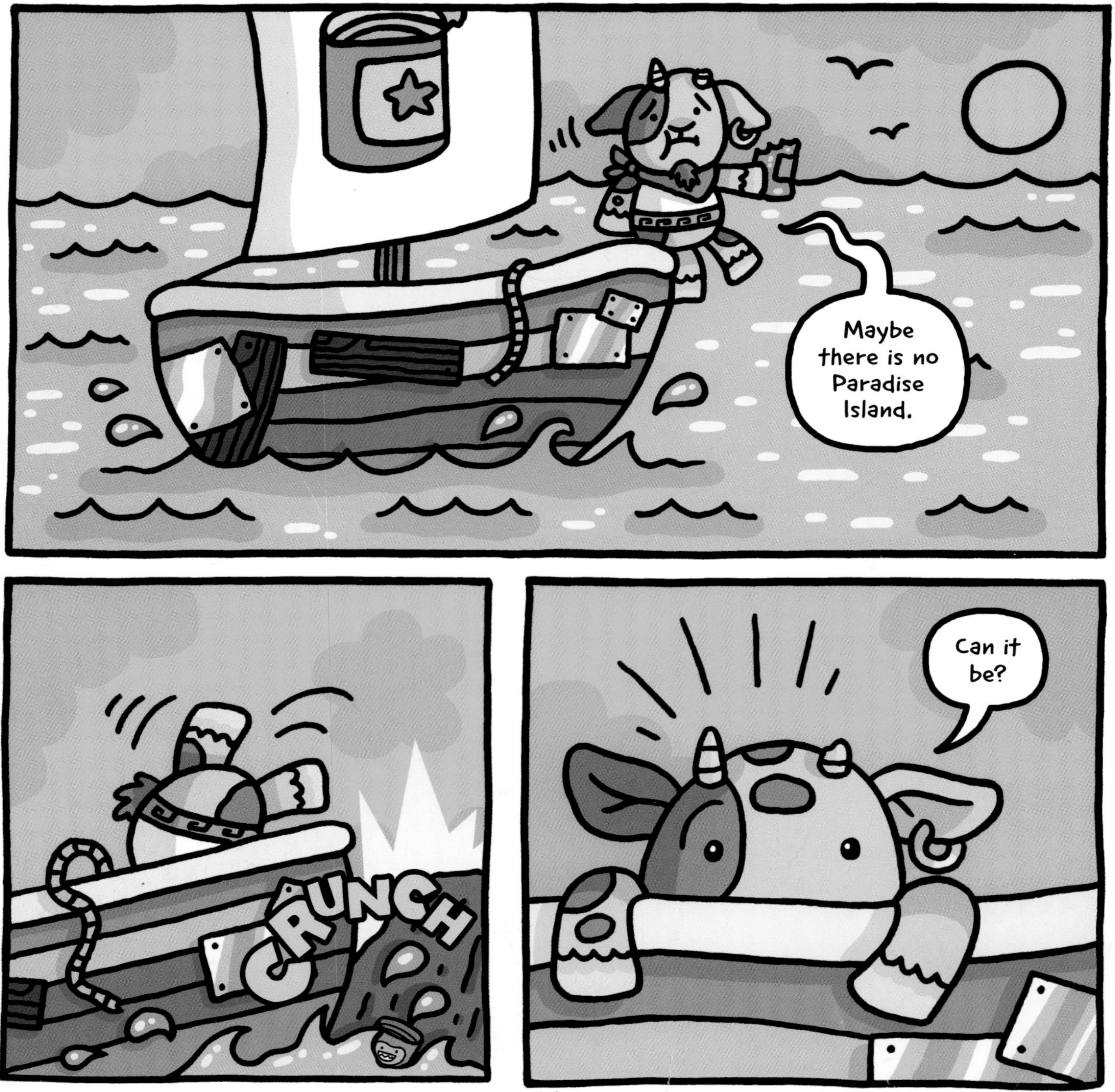
Maybe there is no Paradise Island.
CRUNCH
Can it be?

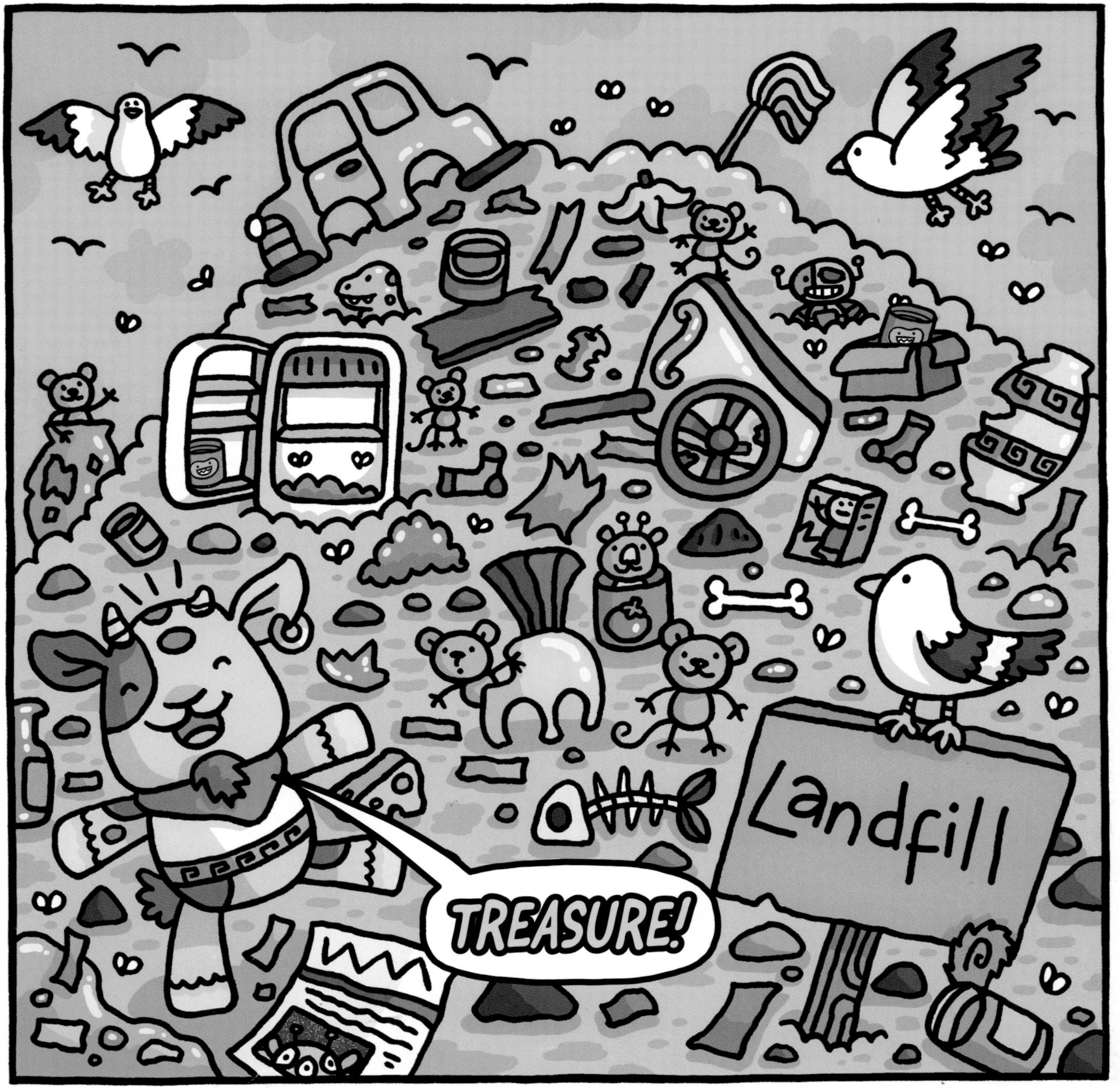
Landfill
TREASURE!

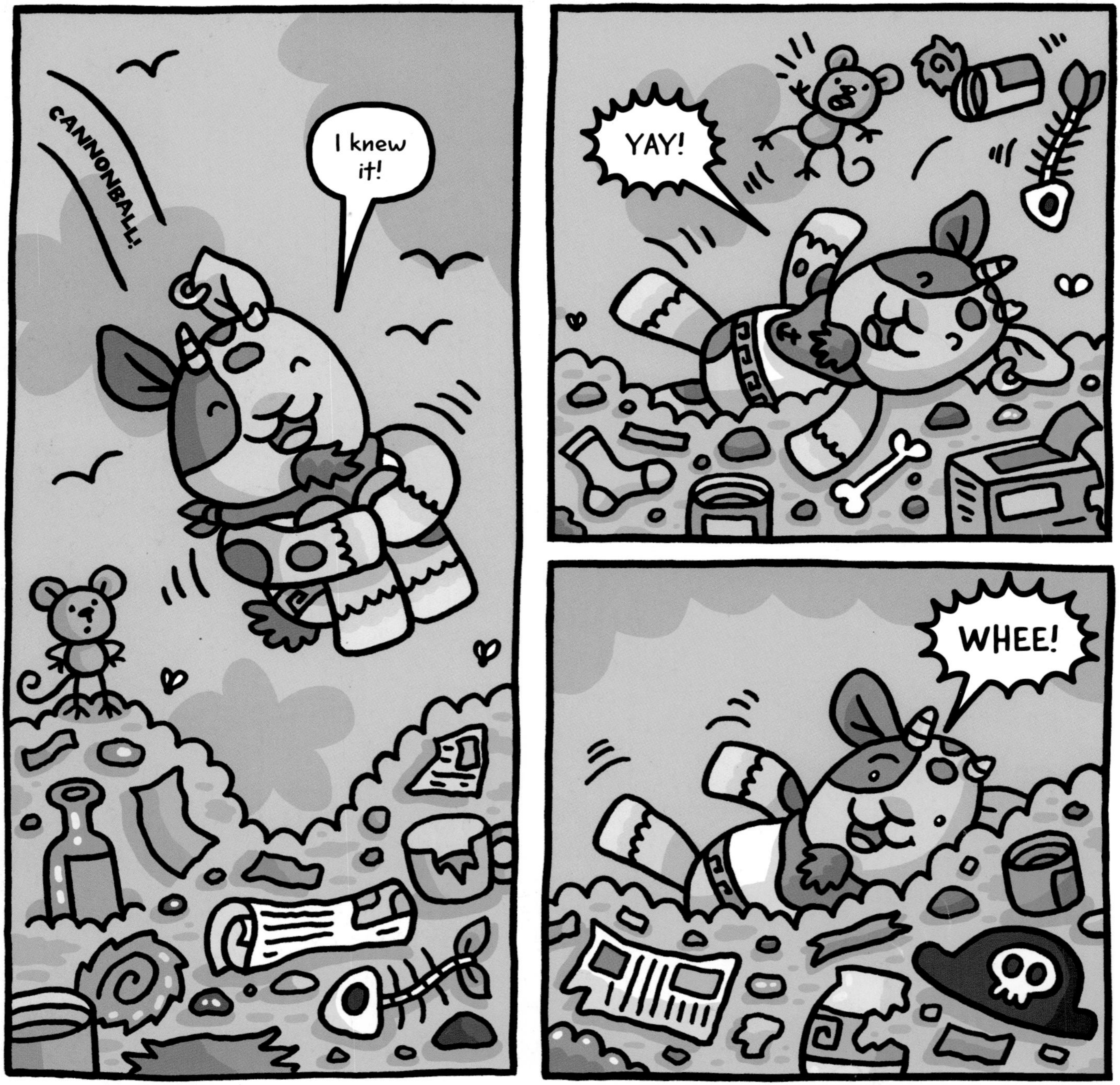
CANNONBALL!
I knew it!
YAY!
WHEE!

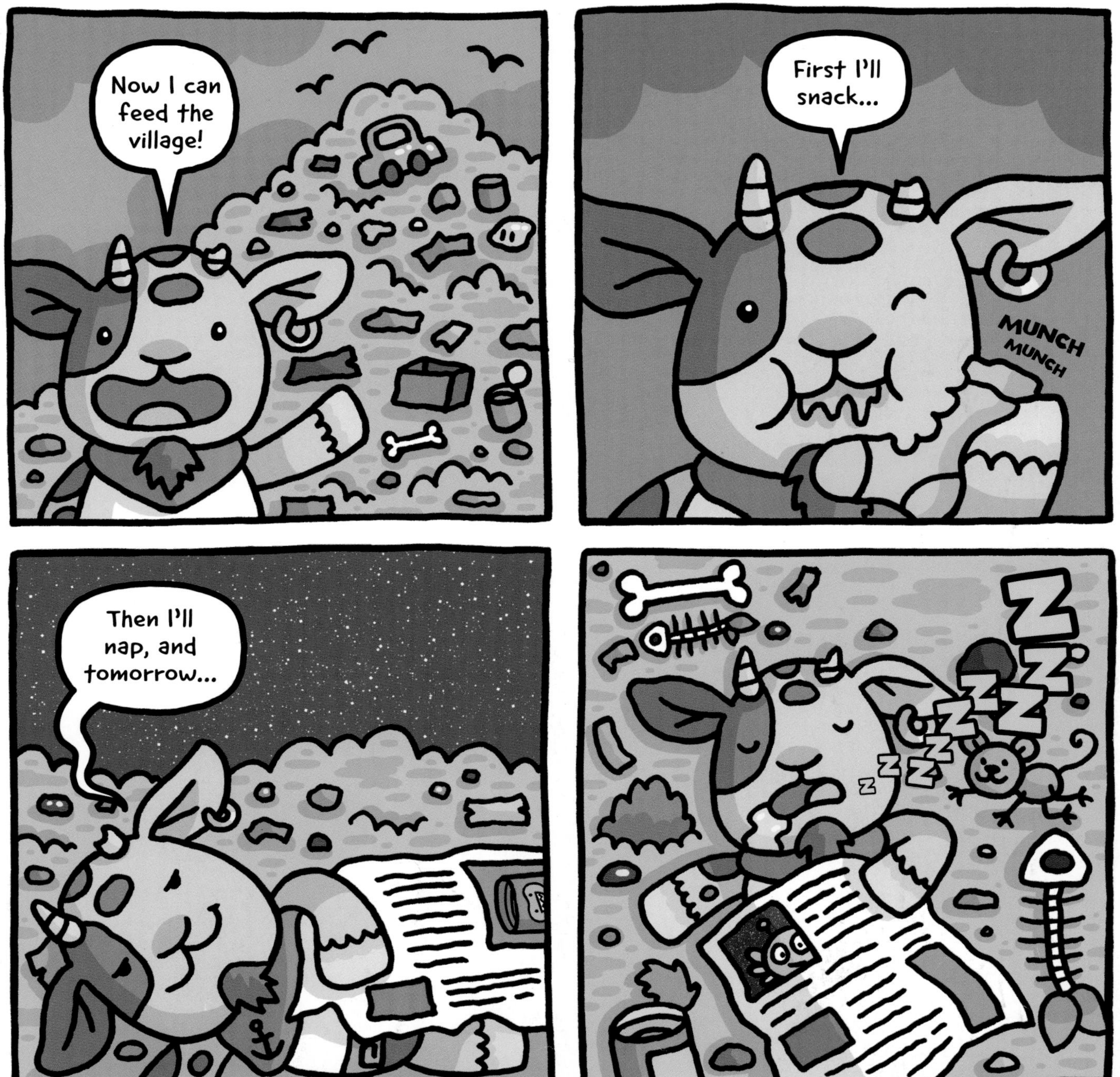
Now I can feed the village!
First I'll snack...
MUNCH
MUNCH
Then I'll nap, and tomorrow...

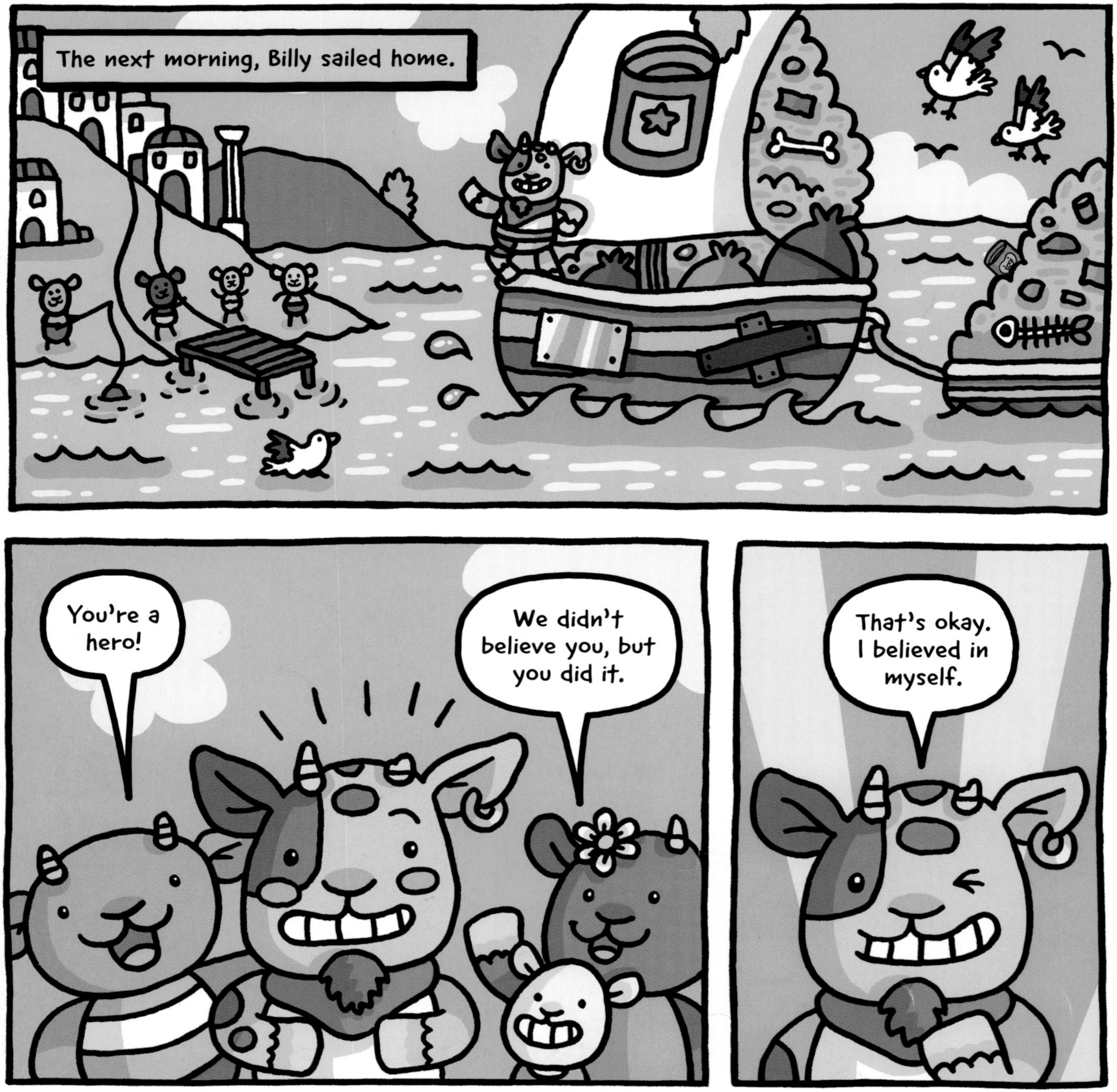
The next morning, Billy sailed home.
You're a hero!
We didn't believe you, but you did it.
That's okay. I believed in myself.

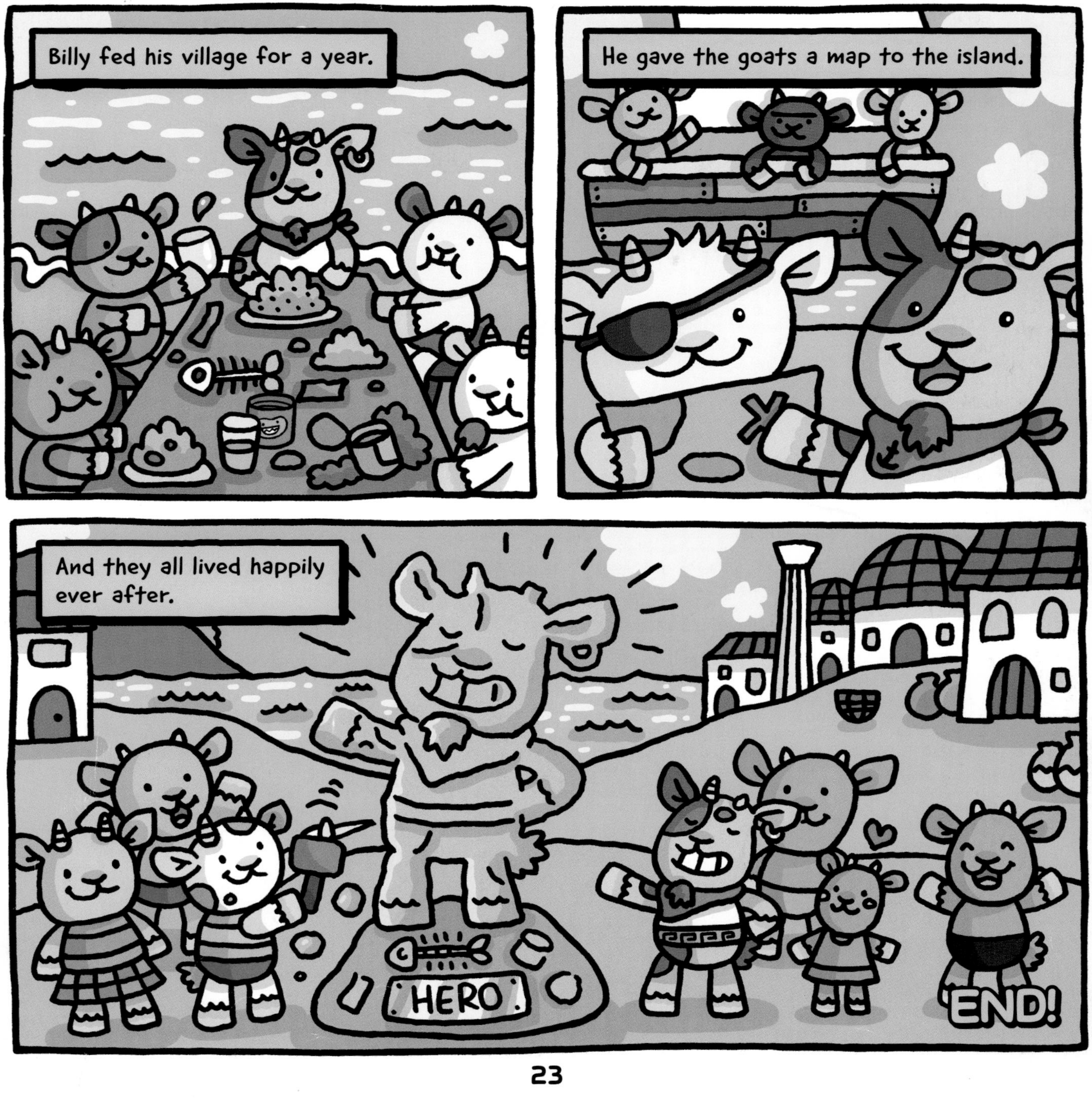
Billy fed his village for a year.
He gave the goats a map to the island.
And they all lived happily ever after.
HERO
END!

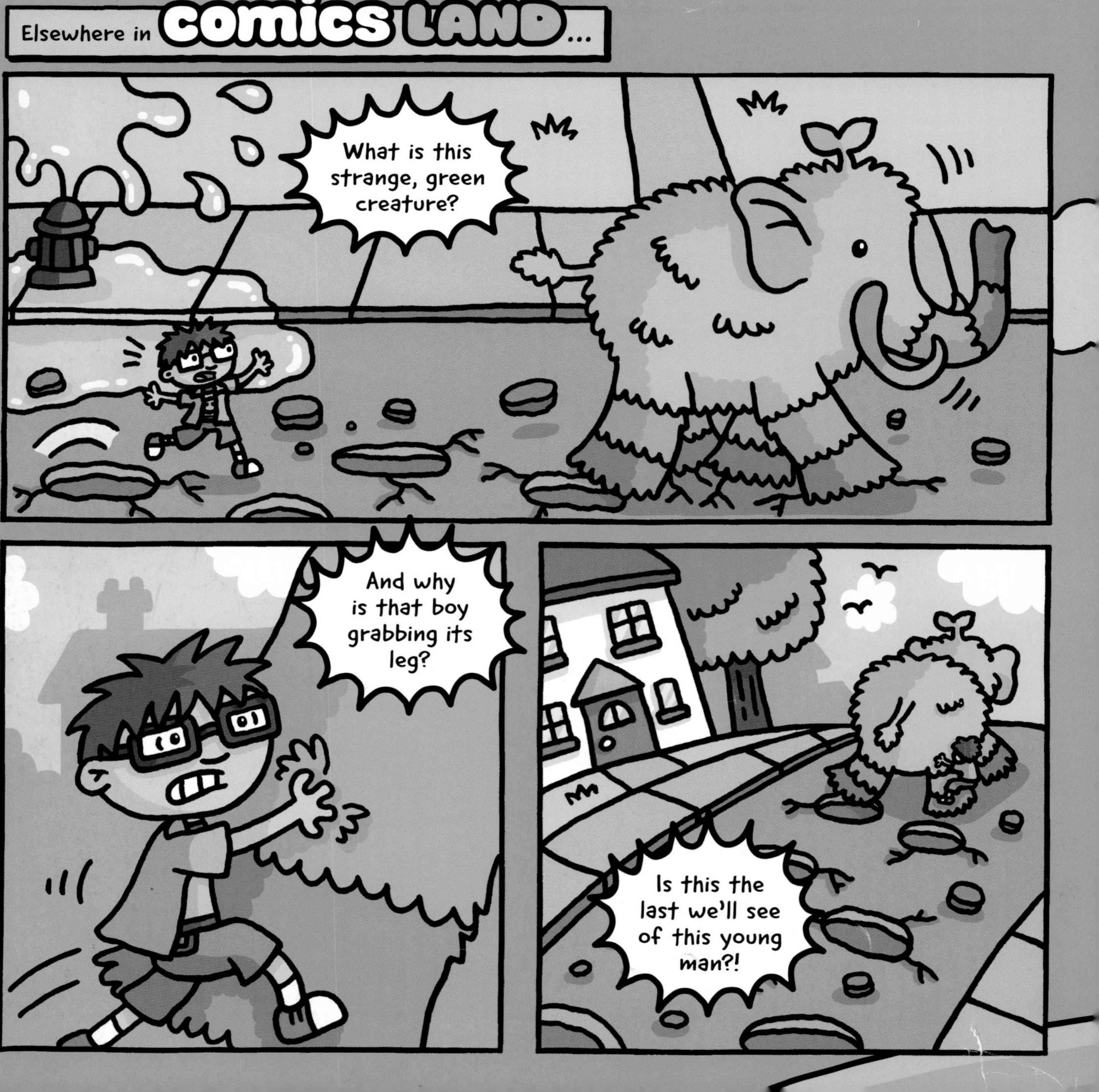
Elsewhere in COMICS LAND...
What is this strange, green creature?
And why is that boy grabbing its leg?
Is this the last we'll see of this young man?!

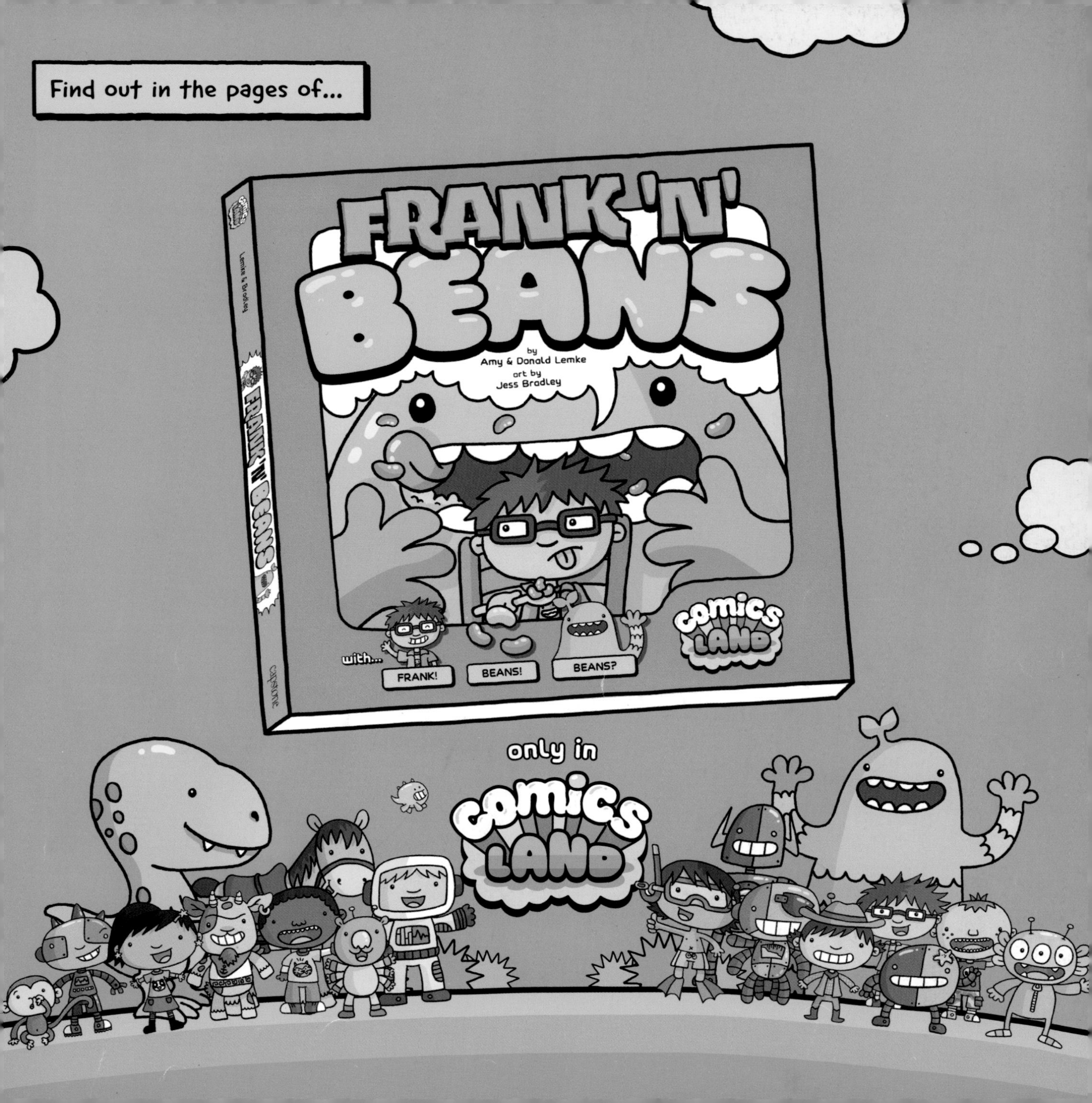
Find out in the pages of...
FRANK 'N' BEANS
by
Amy & Donald Lemke
art by
Jess Bradley
with...
FRANK!
BEANS!
BEANS?
COMICS LAND
Lemke & Bradley
FRANK 'N' BEANS
capstone
only in
COMICS LAND

WORD POWER!

CYCLOPS (SYE-klops) — a giant in Greek myths with a single eye in the middle of the forehead

GARBAGE (GAR-bij) — food or things thrown away

HYDRA (HYE-druh) — a monster with many heads in Greek myths

MINOTAUR (MIN-uh-tawr) — a monster in Greek myths shaped half like a bull and half like a man

PARADISE (PA-ruh-dise) — a place that is considered extremely beautiful and that makes people feel happy and contented

SURVIVED (sur-VIVED) — stayed alive through or after a dangerous event

TREASURE (TREZH-ur) — gold, jewels, money, or other valuable things that have been collected or hidden

Why do you think Billy has an empty can on the mast of his ship?

The cyclops is mad! List at least three clues from the picture that tell us that he is mad.

What do the lines around Billy's feet show?

GOAT ON A BOAT PRESENTS

GAME TIME!

Every box, balloon, and burst in a comic has a special name and job. Can you match the object with its name?

A. SOUND BURST

B. SURPRISE LINES

C. EXCITEMENT BALLOON

D. WORD BALLOON

E. MOTION LINES

F. SOUND EFFECT

G. NARRATIVE BOX

H. THOUGHT BALLOON

1=D, 2=H, 3=G, 4=A, 5=E, 6=B, 7=F, 8=C

Unscramble the letters to reveal words from the story.

1.	ERHO	5.	SRREEATU
2.	LNISDA	6.	LODG
3.	SRONTEM	7.	VELISR
4.	ATOG	8.	ARGGEAB

1. HERO, 2. ISLAND, 3. MONSTER, 4. GOAT, 5. TREASURE, 6. GOLD, 7. SILVER, 8. GARBAGE

FIND THE TIN CAN!

Billy's favorite thing to snack on is red and green cans like this one. Take another look at the story and find the **11** cans hidden throughout the pages.

GOAT ON A BOAT

PRESENTS

DRAW COMICS!

Want to make your own comic about Billy's journey? Start by learning to draw the little goat. Comics Land artist Jess Bradley shows you how in six easy steps!

You will need:

1.

2.

Draw in pencil!

3.

4.

5.

Outline in ink!

6.

Color!

JOHN SAZAKLIS

AUTHOR

John Sazaklis spent part of life working in a family coffee shop, the House of Donuts. The other part, he spent drawing and writing stories. He has illustrated Spider-Man books and written Batman books for HarperCollins. He has also created toys used in *MAD Magazine*.

JESS BRADLEY

ARTIST

Jess Bradley is an illustrator living and working in Bristol, England. She likes playing video games, painting, and watching bad films. Jess can also be heard to make a high-pitched "squeeeee" when excited, usually while watching videos clips of otters or getting new comics in the mail.

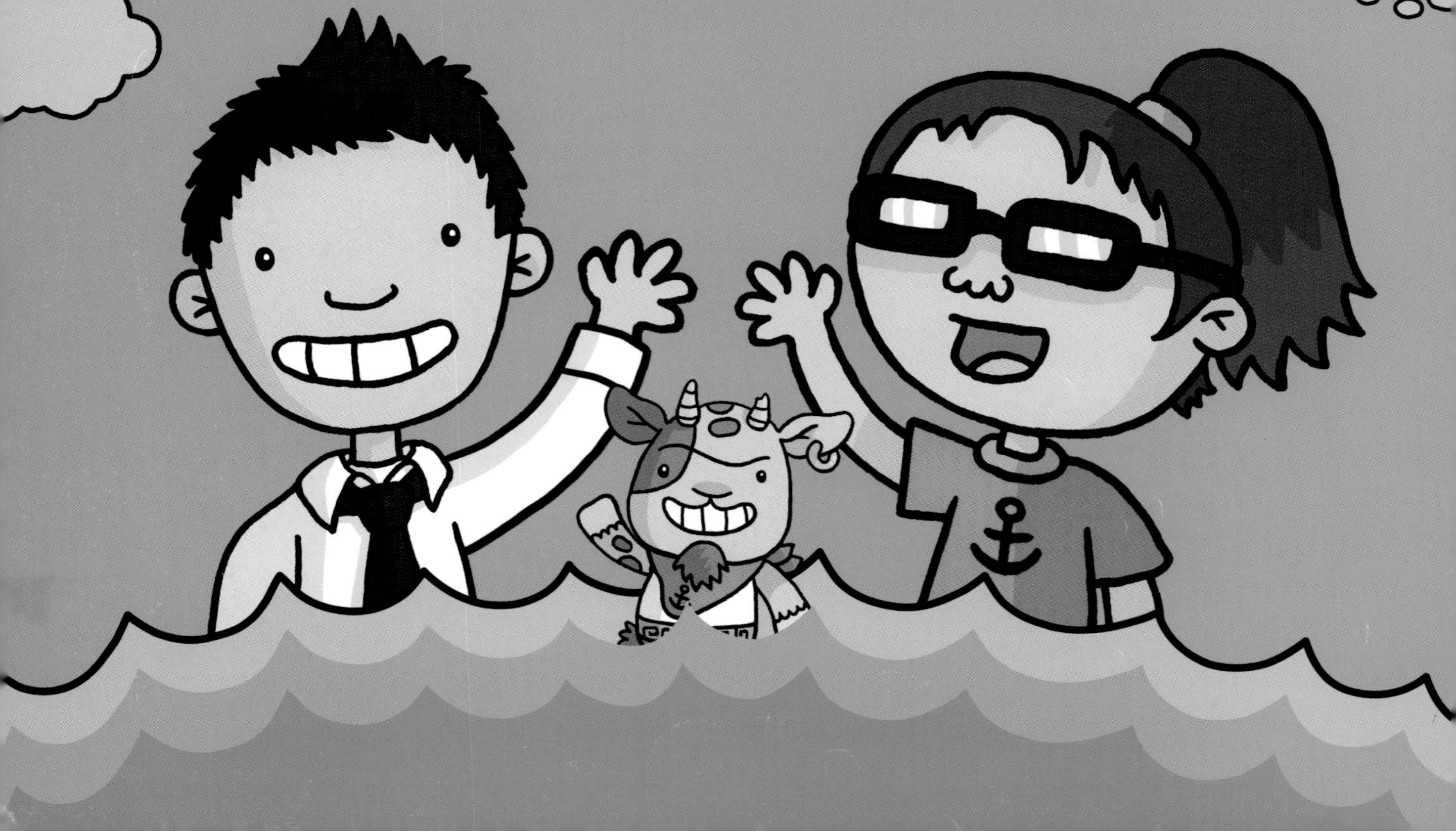